Scruffy's
Museum Adventure

Written by
Claudia Logan

Illustrated by
Jozeph Zaremba

Museum of Fine Arts, Boston

10 9 8 7 6 5 4 3 2

First published in 1996 by the
Museum of Fine Arts, Boston
Department of Retail Publications
295 Huntington Avenue
Boston, Massachusetts 02115

ISBN 0-87846-432-8

Printed and bound in Hong Kong

Designed by Ars Agassiz

For my mother.
—C.L.

For my family.
—J.Z.

"Mom, where's Scruffy?"
"I thought you had him!"
"He was right here!"

"Could he have gone into the Museum?"
"Oh, Dad, dogs aren't allowed in the Museum!"
"But you know Scruffy — he never reads signs."

"How did that dog get in here?"
"Same way you did — the main entrance."

"Mom, how come we didn't bring Bowser?"

NOW THIS IS MY KIND OF COUCH. A NICE OLD COUCH WITH PILLOWS. NAP TIME!

BUT FOR A MODERN DOG - THIS ONE WOULD BE JUST RIGHT.

"A dog is loose in the Museum? I'll try to find him, but remember —
he's got four legs and I've only got two."

"Don't let him escape! He's headed for the garden."

"There he is! We've got him now!"

"Does he belong to you? We've been chasing this guy through the whole museum. I think he's seen everything."

"Scruffy — there you are! We've been looking everywhere for you! Let's go home."

Scruffy's Favorites

A statue of the Greek poet and musician *Orpheus* and the three-headed dog *Cerberus*.

Thomas Crawford (American, 1811/13?–1857)
Gift of Mr. and Mrs. Cornelius Vermeule III
1975.800

A painting called *Still Life with Bread, Ham, Cheese and Vegetables,* around 1770.

Luis Melédez (Italian, worked in Spain, 1716–1780)
Margaret Curry Wyman Fund 39.40

A portrait of *The Postman Joseph Roulin,* 1888.

Vincent Van Gogh (Dutch, worked in France, 1853–1890)
Gift of Robert Treat Paine, II 35.1982

A *Grecian Couch.*

John Finlay (American, 1777–1851) or
Hugh Finlay (American, 1781–1831)
Gift of Mr. and Mrs. Amos B. Hostetter, Jr.,
Anne and Joseph P. Pellegrino,
Mr. and Mrs. Peter S. Lynch, Mr. William N. Banks,
Jr., Eddy G. Nicholson, Mr. and Mrs. John Lastavica,
Mr. and Mrs. Daniel F. Morley,
and Edward J. Holmes Fund 1988.530

A contemporary chair.

Dale Broholm (American 1956–)
Gift of Alan Dinsfriend 1986.676

Egyptian statues.

A sculpture called *Narcisse Noir.*

Katharine Lane Weems (American, 1899–1989)
Samuel Putnam Avery Fund 27.300

A painting of *Boston Common at Twilight,* 1885–1886

Childe Hassam (American, 1859–1935)
Gift of Miss Maud E. Appleton 31.952

A sculpture of *Abraham Lincoln*

Daniel Chester French (American, 1850–1931)
Anonymous gift in Memory of
Beatrice Webb Perrin 48.1

Japanese armor.

And, of course, Scruffy's ancestor.

Illustrated by Randolph Caldecott (English, 1846–1886)
for a book called *The Complete Collection of Pictures and Songs,* London, 1887. Gift of Miss Ellen T. Buchard 1956.885